PARENT-CHILD-CONNECT (P2C)

BOOK SERIES

This book is dedicated to my beautiful wife and children. I love you all!

To my wonderful family and support system,

you guys rock!

And to those from The Shadow (no matter who, what, or where that may be),

YOU CAN do it... I believe in you!

CROW
FROM THE
SHADOW

BY OLAOLU OGUNYEMI

ILLUSTRATED BY

JOSHUA OGUNYEMI

Hi, I'm Crow.

Crow from The Shadow.

3

The Shadow is a person...

or maybe a thing...

or a place.

The Shadow tells me
who to be,
how to go,
and where to stay.

I wear all black,
although my favorite color is blue.

6

Black cap. Black shades.
Yep, that's what The Shadow tells me to do.

7

School is easy,
I can always get an "A."

8

Buuut, why would I do that?
That's not The Shadow's way.

9

I love sunsets on the beach
while enjoying a nice book to read.

Buuut, The Shadow said reading is boring,
so that hobby is not for me.

11

I love flying like the wind
while I chat with my friends.

12

Buuut, The Shadow said that I am a loner,
so I just play pretend.

13

I really love sports!
Basketball is what I love to play.

Buuut, The Shadow said, "Don't play sports."
So, I just sleep all day.

15

I had a dream that I earned a degree and decided to protect and serve.

Buuut, The Shadow told me that I would never overcome life's hills and curves.

17

I am an amazing architect.
I built an Eiffel Tower with toothpicks.

Buuut...WAIT...
The Shadow told me that
I can only dig a ditch?!

19

I have climbed a mountain,
and I have sped around curves.
I have greeted many friends,
and I have read hundreds of words.

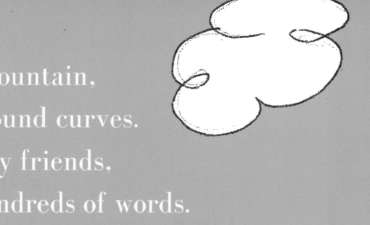

I have great manners,
and I am excellent at school.
Why should I listen to The Shadow
when The Shadow tells untruths?

21

I CAN BE A SUCCESS
AND EVEN CHOOSE A MATE!

WHO GAVE THE SHADOW
THE POWER TO CONTROL <u>MY</u> FATE?

I will move forward
and become all that I can be.

Only one can determine my future.

...atulations

duates!

That one is *me!*

THE
END

DID YOU KNOW...?

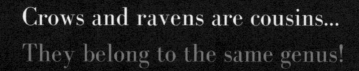

Crows and ravens are cousins...
They belong to the same genus!

Crows are really smart because of
their <u>HUGE</u> brains!

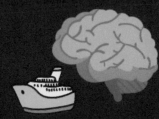

Crows from different places speak
different languages...
just like humans!

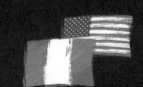

Older crow siblings can help their parents
raise newborns!

Crows have great memory and can
remember your face...
Better mind your manners next time
you see a crow!

CONTINUE THE CONVERSATION...

How would you describe
Crow?

How would you describe
The Shadow?

What changed throughout
the story?

What is the most important
part of the story?

lzgphotography.com   @lzgphotography

Parent-Child-Connect (P2C)

Parent—Child—Connect (P2C) is a book series that assists parents in connecting with their children to teach valuable life lessons.

Our P2C series provides fun, educational, and exciting ways to connect with your children while tackling topics like self-worth, overcoming adversity, developing a winning personality, finances, AND MORE!

Grab your copies today and begin teaching life lessons while creating memorable experiences with your children!

PARENT-CHILD-CONNECT (P2C)
BOOK SERIES
★ ★ ★ ★ ★

Meet the
Author & Illustrator

Olaolu & Joshua Ogunyemi

(Yep, we are brothers!)

Author

Illustrator

A loving husband, Father, teen mentor, and U.S. Marine Officer, Olaolu has a deep passion for working with children fueled by an unending supply of energy and imagination! Since he was young, Olaolu has been nicknamed the "life of the party" because he pours his exuberant personality into every story that he tells. As the fifth of six children, he is intimately familiar with the bond that is forged during quality storytime; thus, Olaolu was inspired to start writing children's stories to help create loving and memorable family moments.

Olaolu writes in a simple, easily understandable language, and an entertaining style that keeps families hooked to his books while learning vital lessons about virtues and sparking a continuing conversation.

Olaolu is a frequent traveler and in his free time, he enjoys playing music, exercising, writing, and spending time with his family.

"Josh O." is a devoted husband, dad, mentor , author, and entrepreneur. He is proof that faith, courage, and determination will outlast even the toughest challenges. His story has inspired many, exemplifying spiritual and mental toughness, defying every challenge he's had to face.

Despite losing a child, extended periods of unemployment, failures, financial problems, the everyday pressures of marriage and fatherhood, and raising a child with special needs, he has become a champion of challenging situations and encourages others to do the same.

Josh's book "**tough times don't last, TOUGH PEOPLE DO**" is a must read! Josh shows you how to turn your hard times Into THRIVING times with just 9 Key habits.

"IMAGINE YOU HAD A BLUEPRINT--
A guide to help you during hard times. YOU can come out ON TOP!
You just need the tools to help get you there."
-Josh O

Connect with Olaolu
www.parent-child-connect.com

"tough times don't last, TOUGH PEOPLE DO"
Available now at
https://excelu.groovepages.com/ttdlebook/index

CPSIA information can be obtained
at www.ICGtesting.com
Printed in the USA
BVHW020717190821
614647BV00004B/14